For Darcie, who (sort of) changed her mind about spiders. —R. K.

For my husband, Rob and for my kind math teacher, Mr. Ward, who always let me draw mice in my math books —A. P.

STERLING CHILDREN'S BOOKS
New York

An Imprint of Sterling Publishing Co., Inc.
1166 Avenue of the Americas
New York, NY 10036

Text © 2019 Robin Koontz
Cover and interior illustrations © 2019 Amy Proud

ISBN 978-1-4549-2356-5

Distributed in Canada by Sterling Publishing Co., Inc.
c/o Canadian Manda Group, 664 Annette Street
Toronto, Ontario M6S 2C8, Canada
Distributed in the United Kingdom by GMC Distribution Services
Castle Place, 166 High Street, Lewes, East Sussex BN7 1XU, England
Distributed in Australia by NewSouth Books
University of New South Wales, Sydney, NSW 2052, Australia

For information about custom editions, special sales, and premium and corporate purchases, please contact Sterling Special Sales at 800-805-5489 or specialsales@sterlingpublishing.com.

Manufactured in China

Lot #:
2 4 6 8 10 9 7 5 3 1
01/19

sterlingpublishing.com

Cover and interior design by Irene Vandervoort
The artwork for this book was created with pencil and acrylic paint.

BUG

WRITTEN BY
Robin Koontz

ILLUSTRATED BY
Amy Proud

STERLING CHILDREN'S BOOKS
New York

Bug was not called Bug because she was
little like a bug, even though she was.

And she was not called Bug because she
ran fast like a bug, even though she did.

Bug was called Bug because she loved every
winging, singing, crawling, biting, stinking,
slinking, stinging bug there was.

Bug liked to draw bugs more than
do anything else in the world.

Especially math.

When Mrs. Muskie talked to the class about math, Bug doodled bugs in her sketchbook and stared out the window.

She couldn't wait to race outside to the open field and look for new bugs to draw.

Mrs. Muskie shook her head, whooshing her cloud of curly hair.

"Bug, you must spend less time doodling and more time on math!"

One day, Mrs. Muskie made an announcement to the class: "If everyone does well on the big math test tomorrow, we'll plan a trip to the science museum!"

Mrs. Muskie smiled.

Bug frowned.

Bug's friend Jasper was the only kid in class who would walk home with her. He didn't mind when she shoved some new kind of insect in his face.

"You *have* to pass the big math test," said Jasper. "You've *always* wanted to go to that awesome bug room at the science museum!"

Bug sighed. "I'll do my best. Walk the rest of the way without me. I have to spend time on math."

Bug wandered to the wild field by the school. She tried to think about math, but she heard honeybees buzz and katydids chirp. Gnats tickled Bug's nose, and dragonflies fanned her face. **A** butterfly landed on a flower.

Bug doodled it in her sketchbook. She drew spots on the butterfly's wings.

Then Bug shook her head. "I must spend less time doodling and more time on math!"

She spotted shiny black ants marching down a tiny path, each carrying a seed.

Bug couldn't help herself . . . she doodled the busy ants.

Suddenly a beetle crashed through the parade of ants. Some of the ants dropped their seeds and chased the beetle away. Bug drew the whole scene.

Bug shook her head again. "I MUST spend less time doodling and more time on math."

Bug spotted a cluster of crickets on a rotting log.
They were huddled in two small groups.

She turned a page in her sketchbook
and doodled the crickets.

Then Bug shook her head again. "I must spend **LESS** time doodling and **MORE** time on math."

She read over her math homework. But it still didn't make any sense. Bug sighed. Then she looked at her doodles.

The butterfly had 3 spots on each wing. Bug counted 6 spots.

Bug looked at the ants. There were 20 ants carrying seeds. Then 6 ants dropped their seeds to chase the brown beetle. *Now there are 14 ants carrying seeds*, thought Bug.

Bug counted the groups of crickets clustered on her last sketch. *4 + 3 = 7*, thought Bug.

Bug squealed. "That's math! I'm doing math!"

She doodled a group of 5 more crickets. "Now there are **12** crickets!" cried Bug. "Math is easy! I will pass the big test!"

Bug remembered reading somewhere that crickets brought good luck. She scooped up a handful and released them inside her lunch box. **As** she hurried home, she whispered to them, "I'll bring you back here right after the test tomorrow."

The next day, Mrs. Muskie passed out the math test. "Please raise your hand when you're done. Good luck!"

The first problem was 7 + 8 = __.
Bug doodled a butterfly. She drew 7 spots on
the first wing and 8 spots on the other wing. 15!

The next problem was 11 - 8 = __. Bug doodled 11 ants
carrying seeds. She crossed out 8 seeds. She counted the seeds
that were left. The answer was 3! Bugs made math easy!

BONUS!

SHOW YOUR THINKING!

6 - 4 + 7 - 6 =

Bug flew through the test. She doodled bugs for every question. At last, Bug got to the BONUS question. Bug had never, ever tried the BONUS question. Now was her big chance.

6 - 4 + 7 - 6 = __ (Show your thinking.)

All those numbers! So many numbers! Bug needed help.

Bug opened her lunch box. She peeked at her lucky crickets. Then Bug started drawing again.

She doodled 6 crickets and crossed out 4. She doodled 7 more crickets next to the remaining ones.

Then she crossed out 6. Bug counted the bugs that were left. Then she did the math: 6 - 4 + 7 - 6 = 3!

She wrote her answer and raised her hand.

Mrs. Muskie walked to Bug's desk
and picked up her test paper.
The lunch box chirped.

Bug looked down just as all the crickets
leaped straight up out of the lunch box . . .

... and into Mrs. Muskie's cloud of hair.

Mrs. Muskie screamed and waved her arms. "Get them off! GET THEM OFF!"

"They think your hair is a field," said Bug calmly. "They are aggregating on you."

"That is a wonderful vocabulary word, Bug!" yelled Mrs. Muskie. "But I AM NOT A FIELD!"

"We have to take them outside," said Bug.

Mrs. Muskie and Bug raced to the empty field. The class followed.

Bug gently gathered the crickets
from Mrs. Muskie's hair and placed
each one back on the log.

Mrs. Muskie shook her hair
and combed through it with
her hands. She took a very
deep breath.

"WHY were there CRICKETS in my classroom, Bug?"

"I was doing math by counting bugs," explained Bug. "And I showed my thinking, like you wanted."

Mrs. Muskie took another very deep breath and looked closely at Bug's test paper. She checked all the answers.

"This is very good work, Bug," she said. "Congratulations!"

The whole class cheered as Mrs. Muskie pulled her special gold pencil from her pocket and wrote a big **A+** on Bug's math test, along with a note.

The next week, Bug and her entire
class went to the science museum.

Bug did **LOTS** of doodling
(and some math, too).

Even Mrs. Muskie spent
time in the Bug Room.

She wore a hat.